Sarah's Surprise

by Nan Holcomb

illustrated by Dot Yoder

JASON & NORDIC PUBLISHERS
HOLLIDAYSBURG, PENNSYLVANIA

Other Turtle Books

Andy Opens Wide
Patrick and Emma Lou
Cookie
A Smile From Andy
Danny and the Merry-Go-Round
Andy Finds a Turtle
How About a Hug

Touch Talker™ is a trademark of the Prentke Romich Company.

Library of Congress Cataloging-in-Publication Data

Holcomb, Nan, 1928—
    Sarah's Surprise / by Nan Holcomb; illustrated by Dot Yoder. p. cm.
    Summary: Six-year-old Sarah, mobile but unable to talk, wants to sing "Happy Birthday" for her mother and is able to provide a birthday surprise with help from her therapist and a new augmentative communication device.

    [1. Mutism—Fiction. 2. Birthdays—Fiction. 3. Mothers and daughters—Fiction.] I.Yoder, Dot, 1921— ill. II. Title.
PZ7.H6972Sar 1990
[E] — dc20

90-4512
CIP
AC

ISBN 0-944727-07-7
Printed in the U.S.A.

For Stephen,
Katie and all our friends
at Old Forge School

"Turn out the lights, Daddy!

Here we come!"

Sarah held the door open!

Sarah's big brother, Brian, brought out
the beautiful cake with lots of candles on it.
Jay and Julie followed with the party
plates.

Everyone sang, "Happy Birthday to you,
Happy Birthday to you,
Happy Birthday, Happy
Birthday,
Happy Birthday, to you!"

Everyone —

except Sarah.

Everyone looked happy.
Everyone —

except Sarah.

Sarah couldn't sing "Happy Birthday."
Signing "Happy Birthday" wouldn't do. It just wouldn't do.

"Sarah!" Mommy said. "Come help me.
You can give everyone some cake." Mom cut
the cake and put some on one of the plates.
"This is for Grandpa."

Sarah took the cake to Grandpa.

"Thank you," he said. "But where's my happy girl? The cake would be much better with a smile from Sarah."

How could you feel like smiling if you couldn't sing 'Happy Birthday', Sarah thought. She did give Grandpa a very small smile, and felt a little better.

The next morning Jay and Julie came in
to watch cartoons. There sat Sarah, on the
floor, coloring a picture of a birthday cake.

"Hey, you're not watching cartoons!" Jay said.

Sarah made a face.

"What's wrong with you?" Julie asked. Sarah pointed to the picture. She wrote 'Mom' with purple crayon.

"What do you want?" Jay asked.

Sarah made the sign for 'I' and 'want'.

"You want Mom?" Jay asked. Sarah gave him a dirty look.

"You want a birthday? a party? a story? a house?. . . a tree? . . . a dinosaur? Jay got silly.

Sarah didn't think it was funny.

"Get serious, Jay," Julie said. "It has
something to do with a birthday party. You
want to say happy birthday?"

Sarah shook her head, 'no'.

"Sing! You want to SING 'Happy
Birthday'!"

Sarah smiled.

"But you can't sing," Jay said.

"Then we'll have to help her find
something she can do," Julie said.

"I know!" Jay shouted and ran to the
closet. He pulled out a sloppy band leader's
hat and an umbrella. "See, we'll sing and you
be the leader!" Jay made funny faces as he
marched around and around.

Julie and Sarah laughed.

"Breakfast is ready. Come and get it,"
Mom called.

Monday morning Sarah still felt unhappy. She looked out the school bus window and wondered, how can I sing 'Happy Birthday'? She had thought and thought. Julie had thought and thought.

Sarah still felt sad when she went to speech therapy.

"Why the sad face?" Miss Kwon asked.

Sarah tried to tell Miss Kwon about the party and how much she wanted to sing, "Happy Birthday."

She touched the sad face on the picture board.

She touched the picture of the grandfather.

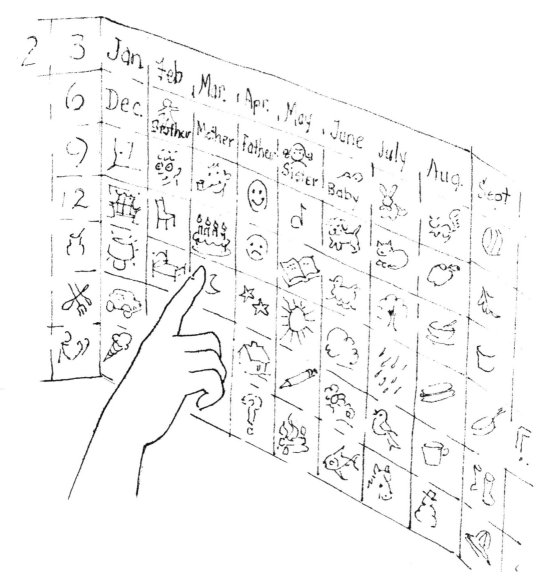

She touched the picture of the birthday cake.

Miss Kwon asked many questions. Sarah nodded her head 'yes' or shook her head 'no'.

At last Miss Kwon understood.

Miss Kwon turned to the computer and touched a picture. The computer said, "Happy Birthday!"

Sarah shook her head. Saying 'happy birthday' wasn't enough for a party! She **had** to sing it!

"If you stop looking sad and think, you would remember that I have a surprise for you today," Miss Kwon said.

The sad look left Sarah's face. She did remember! After weeks of using touch and talk toys, and a computer, she was to have her very own to use at school and at home.

Miss Kwon put a bright new Touch Talker™ on the table in front of Sarah.

"I've put in the words we'll be needing from the picture board, but I had no idea we'd be needing to sing so soon," Miss Kwon said.

Sarah smiled and touched 'mother' on the picture board, then 'December' and '10'.

Miss Kwon said, "That will be easy. I'll even put in a Christmas song if you like."

"A Christmas song!" Sarah thought. She pictured herself leading everyone singing "Happy Birthday."

Then Sarah smiled. She pictured herself in front of the Christmas tree singing . . . "Jingle Bells!" The song I like best! she thought.

At last it was December 10th, Mom's
birthday and Sarah felt happy.
Brian and Jay tied balloons on strings.

Sarah and Julie made a big sign that read, "Happy Birthday, Mom!" Brian, Jay and Julie all helped Sarah try out her birthday surprise for Mom!

Sarah pushed her food around her plate and dropped her peas down to the dog when nobody was looking. She felt too excited to eat.

Sarah watched Grandpa take more
turkey. She wondered if he was going to eat
dinner all over again. At last everyone
finished. At last they were ready for cake.

"Turn out the lights, Daddy!" Here we
come!" This time Jay held the door open.

Brian brought out Mom's beautiful cake.
Julie followed with the plates.
Everyone waited.

Sarah felt very excited as she counted,
one-two- three and . . .
touched the Touch Talker.™

Father

Grandma

Grandpa

Brian

Julie

Jay

"Happy Birthday to you,
    "Happy Birthday to you . . ."
Everyone cheered when Sarah started
the birthday song.
    Then everyone joined in and they sang it
together again with Sarah.

"This is the happiest birthday party this family has ever had," Grandpa said and lifted Sarah high in the air.

Sarah smiled. She would sing "Happy Birthday" at every birthday party from now on!